I'll Go to School If...

Bo Flood

illustrated by Ronnie Shipman

Fairview Press
Minneapolis

Library of Congress Cataloging-in-Publication Data

Flood, Nancy Bo.
  I'll go to school if--- / Nancy Bo Flood ; illustrated by Ronnie Walter Shipman.
      p.   cm.
  Summary: Afraid of the first day of school, a boy says that he will attend only if he can go on a rocket or a lion, but his imaginative suggestions are balanced by Mom's practicality.
  ISBN 1-57749-024-X
  [1. First day of school—Fiction. 2. Schools—Fiction. 3. Imagination—Fiction.] I. Shipman, Ronnie, Walter, ill.
  II. Title.
  PZ7.F66181l   1997
  [E]—dc20   96-38691
                                                                                        CIP
                                                                                        AC

Edited by Robyn Hansen
Cover design by Circus Design

First Printing: July 1997
Printed in the United States of America

01 00 99 98 97   7 6 5 4 3 2 1

Published by Fairview Press, 2450 Riverside Avenue South, Minneapolis, MN 55454.

For a current catalog of Fairview Press titles, please call this Toll-Free number: 1-800-544-8207

Publisher's Note: Fairview Press publishes books and other materials related to the subjects of family and social issues. Its publications, including I'll Go to School If . . ., do not necessarily reflect the philosophy of Fairview Hospital and Healthcare Services or their treatment programs.

The paper used in this publication meets the minimum requirements of American National Standard for Information Sciences—Permanence of Paper for Printed Library Materials, ANSI Z329.48-1984.

I will *not* go to school!
Maybe tomorrow, but not today.

School books have long words
with too many letters.
The teacher will say, "Write your name now."
I won't remember how.

I used to be smart,
but that was last week.
Today I might . . .
make a mistake.

Mom frowns.
"It's the rule to go to school."

I jump up on a chair and stamp my feet.
I'll go to school if . . .

I can finish this spaceship
I'm building with cardboard and glue.
Then I'll zoom over the playground,
right over the slides and the swings.
Everyone will stare.

Their mouths will drop open with surprise.
"Look at that kid! Far out, just amazing!"
They'll watch as I parachute right through the roof
and land, smack! on top of my desk.
If I can soar in a spaceship, I'll go.

Mom points to the mess in my room.
"You've used all the glue."

I will *not* go to school!
Maybe tomorrow, but not today.

The big kids will tease
that I'm too short or too tall.
I won't know their names.
Maybe someone will laugh
because I look scared.
I might . . .
even cry.

"It's the rule to go to school," Mom replies.

I shake my head and pout.

I'll go to school if . . .

I can ride on the back of a lion.
Watch! I'll crack a whip high over my head.
My lion will wear a Wild West hat.

Everyone will cheer, "Bravo! How brave!"
If I can ride on a lion, I'll go.

Mom hands me my backpack.
"Remember? The lions left
with the circus last year."

I will *not* go to school!
Maybe tomorrow, but not today.

Girls will wear dresses
that sparkle and twirl.
Boys will have shoes
that run faster than mine.

Someone will tease that my face is the wrong
color or my eyes are not the right shape.
At school I might . . .
wet my pants.

Mom kisses my nose.
"It's the rule to go to school."

I shake my head and explain.
I'll go to school if . . .

I can buy a stretch limousine
that has chocolate cream doughnuts
and a video screen. Honk the horn!

Shine the lights! Just watch as I drive into sight!
No one will laugh.
If I can cruise up in a limo, I'll go.

Mom shakes my piggy bank.
We don't hear a sound.
"You spent all your pennies
on crayons that glow in the dark."

I will *not* go to school!
Maybe tomorrow, but not today.

There are bullies and monsters
with long yellow teeth who will snarl,
"SIT STILL. BE QUIET. GO AWAY."

I'll hide under my desk the whole day.
But what if I forget the right bus
or which way is home?
Mom, what if you forget about me?

Mom circles her arms around me
and squeezes me a hug.
"I'll miss you, and I'm scared, too.
But it's important to go to school."

I look up and whisper,
"Could you come too?"

Mom zips up my coat and reaches for hers.
"There is no rule that mothers can't go to school.
I might need to cry. Most mothers do cry
on the first day of school."

It's okay, Mom, you can walk next to me.
I'll growl like a lion,
and when you open that big school door,
I'll roar like a rocket!
Or maybe I'll hum while
you look for the teacher who's looking for me.

Just remember to hold my hand tight.
It's okay to be scared. I'm a little scared too.
Today is the first day of school and . . .
I'm ready to go!

Hints on Handling First-Day Fears

Talk with the child:

• ASK: Is or was the child afraid of the first day of school? What is or was the child afraid of?

• SHARE: "I remember when I first went to school. I was afraid that . . . ."

• VALIDATE: We all have fears about "first days" and "first times."

•IMAGINE: How would you like to look, what would you wear, and what would you ride on that first day? Draw a picture or write a description.